Race Down the Mountain

Retold by Mary C. Olson
Illustrated by Giannini

Workbook Activities by Betty Glennon, B.S., M.S., Series Consultant

To the Parent

A love of books and good reading habits both begin at home -- from the picture books you shared with your child as a baby to the read-aloud stories he or she continues to enjoy.

Now your son or daughter is beginning to recognize words and read independently! Encouraging your child to read at home will help build confidence and enthusiasm for a skill he or she will use for a lifetime.

Here are some suggestions to help your beginning reader: Be sensitive to your child's abilities. Do not force your child, particularly if he or she is not yet learning to read in school.

- Be patient for 5 seconds so your child can try to sound out an unfamiliar word.

- Have your child skip an unknown word and read the rest of the sentence. Come back to the word and ask, "What word would make sense here?" Talk about it a little.

- Encourage your child to use any phonics skills that have been learned to help say the word, for example; beginning consonant sounds.

- Praise the effort!

- If a word is still unknown, say it for your child so he or she can continue reading.

- Encourage your child to use pictures as clues to words and meanings.

- Occasionally, before turning a page, ask your child to predict what will happen next. Praise his or her creative thinking.

- Help your child relate the story to his or her own experiences.

A GOLDEN® BOOK
Western Publishing Company, Inc.
Racine, Wisconsin 53404

Long ago and far away, there was a little train engine.

It was his job to take the cars down the  each day.

mountain

Each day, he rang his bell

and  chugged out of the little town with his cars.

One day, as the little engine went by, the sheep and goats ran up to him.

"Stop, stop!" said the sheep and goats.
"You've lost . . . you've lost . . ."

The little engine rang his bell at them. He said to himself, "What have I lost? A race?"

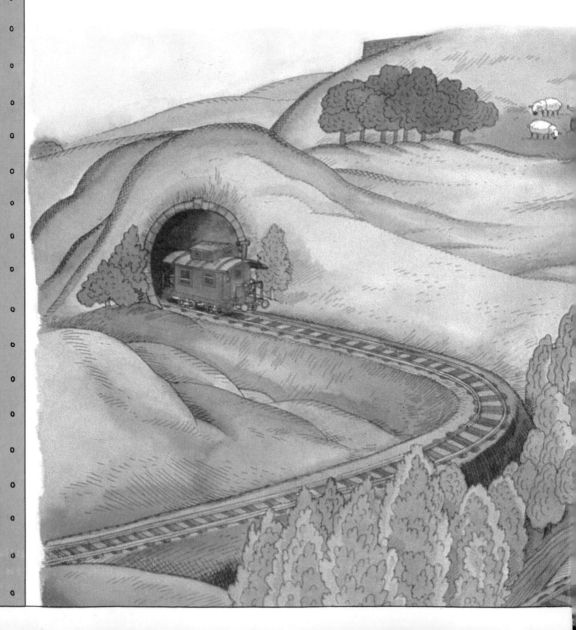

He did not want to lose a race, so he  as fast as he could.

chugged

The little engine rang his bell at the chickens and ducks as he went by. The chickens and ducks said, "You've lost . . . you've lost . . ."

He whistled at the chickens and ducks and went very, very fast.

Down the mountain, the little engine went!

He saw some pigs in the mud. The little engine rang his bell at them.

His bell made the pigs look up from the mud. "You've lost . . . you've lost . . ."

The little engine went down the ⛰ mountain as fast as he could go.

When he was all the way down the mountain, he came to the sea. He still went fast.

Some men were fishing with nets in the
sea. The little engine rang his bell
at the men. But the men just said,
"You've lost . . . you've lost . . ."

At last, the little engine was almost at the end of his trip. He was sad.

"The sheep and the goats, the ducks and the chickens, the pigs and the men all say that I lost. What kind of race have I lost? And who won?"

As the little engine came into the town, he saw what the sheep and goats had seen. He saw what the ducks and chickens had seen. He saw what the pigs in the mud had seen. He saw what the men with their nets had seen.

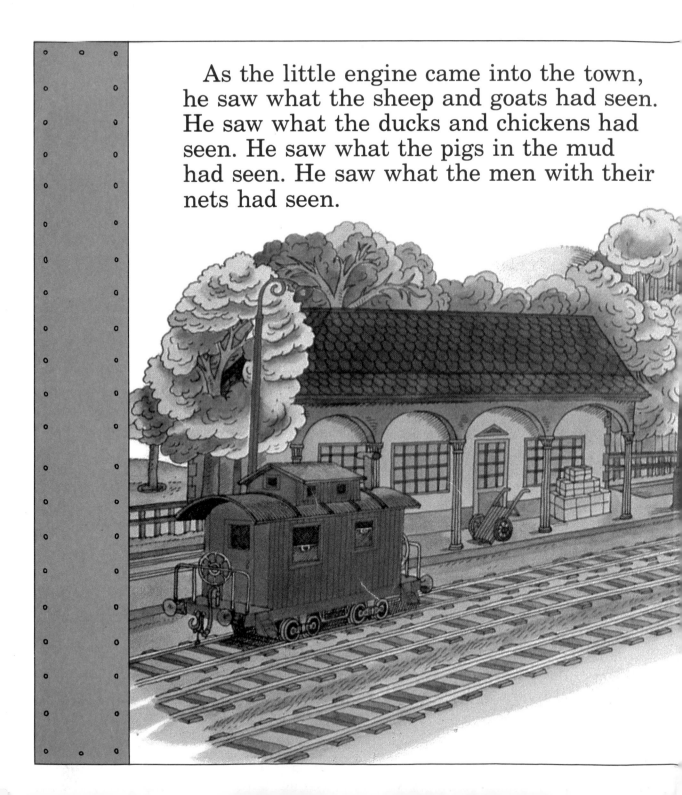

The little engine had not been in a race at all! What he had lost was his red caboose!

The goats and sheep, the ducks and chickens, the pigs and men had all said, "You've lost . . . you've lost your red caboose!"

His red caboose had come down the mountain the other way — all by itself! The little engine was happy.

"I have not lost a race!" he said. "And now I have my red caboose."

"But the next time the goats and sheep, ducks and chickens, pigs and men want to tell me something, I will listen to all of it!"